KT-512-142

Goldilocks
and the
Three Bears

illustrated
by
CHRIS RUSSELL

based on a traditional folk tale

Once upon a time, there were three bears who lived in a little house right in the middle of the forest.

There was great big Father Bear, and medium-sized Mother Bear, and little tiny Baby Bear.

Honey

One morning, Mother Bear made a big pot of porridge and put it into three bowls for breakfast.

But the porridge was much too hot to eat.

"We will leave it to cool while we go for our early morning walk," said Father Bear. "When we come back, it will be just right." So off they went into the forest.

As soon as she saw the porridge, naughty Goldilocks rushed over to taste it. "I do feel rather hungry," she said.

But the porridge in Father Bear's big bowl was still too hot. And the porridge in Mother Bear's medium-sized bowl was lumpy.

At last Goldilocks tried Baby Bear's porridge. It was just right, so she ate up every spoonful!

After that, Goldilocks decided
that she would like to sit down.
But Father Bear's big chair was
much too high.

Next she sat in Mother Bear's
medium-sized chair.
"This one is much
too hard!" she
grumbled.

At last she found
Baby Bear's tiny
chair. It wasn't too
high. It wasn't too
hard. It was just
right!

Goldilocks leaned back happily in
Baby Bear's chair. But she was far
too heavy. With a *creak* and a
crack, the chair fell to pieces.

Bump! Goldilocks landed in a
heap on the floor. "Well, really!"
she said crossly. "I've had such a
shock, I shall have to lie down."

Before long, the three bears
arrived home from their walk.

"I'm ready for my breakfast *right
now,*" said Father Bear. But when
he got to the table he cried out in
surprise, "Someone's been eating
my porridge!"

"And someone's been eating *my* porridge," said Mother Bear. "I wonder why they didn't like it?"

"They must have liked mine!"
cried Baby Bear, holding his
empty bowl. "Someone's been
eating my porridgc, and they've
eaten it all up!"

"Look!" said Father Bear. "Someone's been sitting in my chair!"

"And someone's been sitting in *my* chair," said Mother Bear.

"Someone's been sitting in my chair," sobbed poor little Baby Bear, "and they've broken it to pieces!"

The three bears began to search
the house. Upstairs, Father Bear
looked around. "Someone's been
sleeping in my bed!" he said.

"And someone's been sleeping in
my bed," cried Mother Bear.

"Oh!" squeaked Baby Bear.
"Someone's been sleeping in my
bed and she's *still here!*"

At the sound of Baby Bear's voice, Goldilocks woke up. The first thing she saw was Father Bear, looking very cross.

Goldilocks jumped up in fright.
She ran down the stairs and out of
the house as fast as she could.

"I don't think she'll trouble us
again," said Father Bear, smiling.

And she never did.

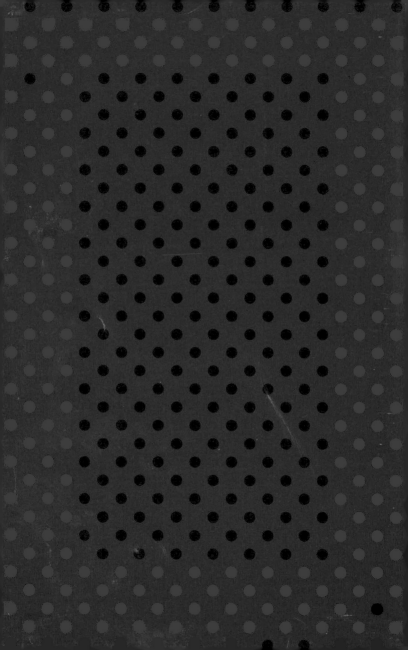